DAUGHTER *of* LIGHT

AN
ORCA
YOUNG
READER

DAUGHTER *of* LIGHT

martha attema

ORCA BOOK PUBLISHERS

Canadian Cataloguing in Publication Data
Attema, Martha, 1949–
Daughter of light

ISBN 1-55143-179-3

1. World War, 1939–1945—Netherlands—Juvenile fiction. I. Title.
PS8551.T74D38 2001   jC813'.54   C2001-910132-5
PZ7.A8664Da 2001

First published in the United States, 2001

Library of Congress Catalog Card Number: 2001086679

Orca Book Publishers gratefully acknowledges the support of our publishing programs provided by the following agencies: the Department of Canadian Heritage, The Canada Council for the Arts, and the British Columbia Arts Council.

Cover design by Christine Toller
Cover and interior illustrations by Stephen McCallum
Printed in Canada

IN CANADA	**IN THE UNITED STATES**
Orca Book Publishers	Orca Book Publishers
PO Box 5626, Station B	PO Box 468
Victoria, BC Canada	Custer, WA USA
V8R 6S4	98240-0468

03 02 01 • 5 4 3 2

Studyguide available at: www.marthaattema.com

To Margaret,

who has told me so much about the war.

Acknowledgements

Reading the war memoirs of Pietsje de Vries-van der Laan inspired me to write this story.

I would like to thank Ann Featherstone for her editorial suggestions. She convinced me to write *Daughter of Light* as a juvenile novel instead of a picture book.

Thank you Maggie de Vries for helping me to shape this story.

I also want to thank Marla Hayes, who never tires of reading my first drafts, Carolyn Saini for reading the story to her students, Margaret Geurtsen Dekker for telling me about her war experiences, Heinz and Helga Schleuting for correcting my usage of the German language, Bea Mooney and Wendy Champaign for their constructive criticism, the members of the North Bay Children's Writers Group for their encouragement and my family for their continuing love and support.

Unwanted Visitors

Bang! Bang!

"*AUFMACHEN!*" The pounding on the door grew louder.

"OPEN UP!" the voice barked again, this time in Dutch.

Ria, her mother and her brother Dirk jumped up from the kitchen table.

Ria held her breath.

Dirk balled his fists.

Mother sent them a stay-calm message

with her eyes. In one swift movement, she grabbed the matches, lit the candle on the table and handed it to Ria.

The pounding continued.

Mother pulled her shawl tight around her shoulders. Supporting her stomach, swollen with their new baby, she opened the door to the front hall. There she paused.

Ria stood close to her mother, paralyzed by fear. She held the candlestick in her trembling hands.

Dirk stood beside her.

It was one of the darkest, coldest days of winter and war in the year 1944. Christmas had passed, the New Year not yet begun. It was not the first time German soldiers had pounded on their door.

"OPEN UP!" the voice shouted, louder this time.

All afternoon they had heard the rumbling of military trucks down the road.

Ria felt for the chain and the locket hidden underneath her woolen sweater. She stared at the door.

Stretching Father's knit sweater over her belly, Mother stepped forward and swung the door open.

Two soldiers stomped inside, carrying a bitter wind. The last one to enter closed the door, crowding them in the narrow, dark hall.

Despite her layers of clothing, Ria shivered. The soldiers' helmets gleamed dimly in the flickering candlelight. Their rifles shone. Their boots smelled of polish and leather.

Dirk, Ria and Mother stood back. What would the soldiers want this time? Ria's heart pounded in her chest. Four-and-a-half years ago, Germany had invaded Friesland, one of the northern provinces in the Netherlands. Her country. Many times since the invasion, the soldiers had pounded on their door. One day they had taken the radio; another time, her mother's silver tea set. Ria tried to push away the memory of the day they had come to take her father away to work in a weapons factory

3

in Germany. Luckily, Father hadn't been home and Dirk had been able to warn him.

Ever since the electricity company had closed down and Father had lost his job, the Nazis had been looking for him. Not just for her father, but for every man between the ages of seventeen and fifty-five. Only men who owned farms or businesses could apply for exemption. Germany needed factory workers to replace the German men who fought at the front.

During the day, Father stayed hidden at a farm outside town. At night he snuck home through dark alleys to be with his family. Under the wooden stairs in the kitchen, they had made a hiding place. The boards of the bottom steps were loose and could be lifted to reveal a small, dark space. Her father had to crouch there, cramped and cold, with his knees pulled up to his chest. If ever the soldiers came during the night, Father had to crawl quickly and silently into his hiding place.

Ria looked at the two soldiers. The

tall one had a grim, bony face. The short one glared at mother with puffy, red eyes. A cold shiver crept up Ria's spine. Thank goodness, Father wasn't home.

The tall one took a step toward Ria. She felt his breath on her face. In the next moment he snatched the candleholder from her hand. She felt the coarse wool of his glove against her skin. Her mouth opened.

Mother gasped.

He pulled the candle from the candle-stick and handed the candle, still burning, back to Ria.

She took it and held it tight. The flame flickered and threw shadows on the people in the crowded hallway.

"Did you forget this?" he growled, waving the candleholder close to Mother's face.

Dirk placed his hand on Mother's arm. Almost twelve, he'd grown as tall as Mother. Ria could hear his angry breathing.

"Remember when we came to collect items that could be melted down to make weapons?" the soldier sneered.

The other soldier opened the door to the left and strode into the front room.

"We need to speak to your husband!" the tall one barked in Mother's face.

"I don't know where he is," Mother answered flatly.

His eyes searched Ria's face.

Without breathing, she shook her head.

The soldier shrugged his shoulders and opened the front door.

He looked bored, Ria thought. The wind blew out the candle.

"Close the door," Mother said. "Since you have stolen our fuel, we cannot afford to let the cold inside."

Ignoring her, the tall soldier waited in the open doorway.

The short soldier glanced at the heavy sideboard in the front room. "Why don't you burn that?" he said with a grin. "It will give you many hours of heat." He turned on his heel, walked into the hall, slapped his buddy's shoulder, and stomped outside.

They could still hear the soldiers laughing after Mother closed the door.

Ria gritted her teeth. Her grandfather had made that sideboard. Into the wood, he had carved birds sitting on branches.

She could feel her mother tremble as they stood in the hallway, listening until the rumbling of the truck faded away.

Gently, Ria guided her mother into the kitchen to the chair by the small, iron stove.

"I hate those stupid soldiers with their ugly rifles!" Ria shuddered with anger. "Why did they take our candleholder? Why do they scare us like that?"

Mother shook her head. "That candlestick belonged to my grandmother."

Ria's hand shook as she put the candle on the kitchen table.

"I wish I was old enough to fight them." Dirk scowled. "I would. I would."

"Shh." Mother placed her hand on Dirk's arm. "I'm glad you're not old enough," she sighed. "If only the Germans would restore the electricity." The lines around her mouth gave her a tired look. "Then, this baby could be born safely." She patted her stomach. "We could turn on the small electric heater, the one we got from Grandmother Ria. And we could boil water on the electric stove top and have enough light to make sure the baby's all right."

"Ria and I will go to the park and collect wood for the stove." Dirk stood with his hand on Mother's shoulder.

He's pretending he's Father, Ria thought. Dirk was only two years older than Ria, but lately he was acting as if he were the man of the house. The way Dirk's blond, stubbly hair stood straight on end, Ria had to admit that he looked exactly like Father.

"What sort of a mayor would take away electricity from his own citizens?" Mother's voice was angry. "Just following orders, I guess. But then, being a Nazi sympathizer, maybe it was all his idea! How does he expect women like me to have our babies in cold, dark houses?"

Ria took a saucer from the counter and placed it on the table. Her mother lit the candle. As the wax dripped into the saucer, the beginning of a plan crept into Ria's head. So the mayor had something to say about the electricity, she thought. Mother pressed the candle into the wax.

"We'd better save the candle," she sighed.

Ria closed her eyes and blew out the flame. As she blew, she wished hard for a way to get their electricity back.

When Mother rose from the chair, she held onto the table for support.

Ria stretched her arms around her mother's stomach.

"We will have light, Mother! Our baby will come into a world full of light."

"Not the whole world." Dirk smiled. "Just enough for our house."

"Thank you, Ria." Her mother smiled through her tears. "What would I do without the two of you?" She winked at Dirk.

Ria's brother shoved the last three branches from the bucket into the stove.

As he opened the tiny door, smoke billowed into the room.

Ria coughed.

"All this thing does is smoke and stink; it doesn't give off any heat," Dirk grumbled.

"You're right." Mother rubbed her arms. "It's so cold in this house. I'm going to lie down. The two of you better go to the park before it gets too dark. Search for anything that will burn in this old stove. Anything."

The War

"I'll race you!" Dirk, all bundled up, stood in the doorway, a bucket in his hand.

"No fair!" Ria cried. Still shaking from the soldiers' visit, she fumbled with the buttons on her winter coat.

"Wait!" A sigh escaped her as the last button went through the hole.

Mother was getting too worn out to do all the housework, so Ria and Dirk made beds, washed floors and windows, peeled potatoes, and gathered wood. They had made games of some of the chores. If she concentrated, Ria could peel a potato in one long ribbon. Dirk tried and tried, but every time the skin broke, he cried out, "This is no job for me. It's a girls' job."

"We're at war, Dirk," Mother laughed. "Boys have to do girls' jobs and girls have to do boys' jobs."

The war. The war. Ria hated the war. That's all the grown-ups talked about. Because of the war, there was no school and no good food; there were no trips, and since the electricity had been cut, they were living in a dark house. The worst of the war was the fear. Ria was always afraid. She feared the terrible things the soldiers did, such as rounding people up and sending them away to camps. She feared that the Nazis might find her father. And she feared that she would never see her best friend Rachel again.

Fighting back tears, Ria grabbed her

wooden basket and stomped after her brother.

Brrr. She shivered. The northwest wind whipped her worn winter coat around the tops of her legs and froze her body to the bone. Ria was tired of searching for wood and branches every day. Lately, so many people came to the park scrounging for firewood that it was getting harder and harder to find anything at all.

More than four years ago, the German leader Adolf Hitler had decided that he wanted to rule the whole world. Germany was the eastern neighbor to the Netherlands. Hitler invaded many other countries before he sent his soldiers, guns and bombs into Holland. The Dutch army tried hard to fight the enemy, but they were forced to surrender after only four days. The Germans took control of the entire country.

At first, life had seemed almost normal. But then food, clothing and fuel had become scarce.

Two weeks ago, the invaders had cut the electricity, meaning no more electric lights or electric cooking. Now Ria's family got what meager heat they could from an old iron stove in the kitchen. They had to use it for cooking too.

Ria remembered when they had had coal for the stove in the front room. She had loved to watch the flames through the small mica windows. The front room had been cozy, even on the coldest winter day. But the Germans had sent all the coal to Germany. They had stolen it. They stole everything. Ria kicked at a stone. It hurt her big toe. The soles of her shoes were starting to come apart, like mouths that opened and closed. Mother had glued cardboard inside her shoes, but on wet days the cardboard and her feet got soaked.

Dirk was waiting at the park gate. Ria looked both ways and crossed the street. Not that there was much traffic, just bicycles, wooden carts, wheelbarrows and baby carriages. The Germans had also stolen all the cars along with the fuel to drive them.

A big, metal sign on the park gate read, *VERBOTEN FÜR JUDEN*.

Every time she saw the sign, Ria felt as if a knife had stabbed right through her heart. How could the Germans make a terrible, crazy rule like that: No Jews allowed? Her best friend Rachel was Jewish. Ria remembered playing in the park with Rachel before the Germans came.

In the park, women, children and old men were everywhere, searching for scraps of wood. She recognized Marijke from her homeschooling class. Ria waved. Marijke lifted a twig in greeting.

The people looked like actors in a play. They crouched, knelt, even crawled across the rough ground, shifting buckets and baskets alongside, dressed in layers and layers of clothing to keep out the biting wind.

Farther on, Ria noticed that a row of poplar trees had disappeared. They had been there yesterday. They must have been cut down during the night. Seeing the park destroyed and bare filled her with sadness.

She caught up with Dirk, who was already filling his pail with branches and strips of bark from the cut-down poplars.

"Somebody got lots of wood during the night." Dirk looked at her. "If the Germans find out who they are, they'll be in trouble."

"I know." Ria nodded. She put down her basket and started picking up bits of bark. Terrified of the soldiers, she also felt anger in her chest when she thought of how they had frightened her family this afternoon. She remembered the feel of the soldier's glove against her skin. The memory of that feeling left her mouth dry.

"Not much wood left!"

Ria turned to see Bram de Boer running toward them. He was the same age as she was. Bram lived on the farm, east of their town, where the children received home-schooling. An axe jogged on his shoulder and a pail swung from his hand. Curls of red hair burst from underneath his toque.

Ria didn't like him. He was a loudmouth.

"Did you see all the military trucks this afternoon?" Bram huffed.

"They came to visit us." Dirk put down his bucket.

"What did they want?" Bram lowered the axe to the ground.

"They wanted to speak to my father." Dirk's face showed anger. "Luckily Father wasn't home. I wish I could get my hands on a gun." He picked up a branch and aimed it in the air as if he were holding a rifle.

"Yeah." Bram copied Dirk. Now both boys aimed at the road.

"Ta-ta-ta-ta!" they shouted.

Ria turned away from the boys. She picked up her basket. It wasn't even half full. Nowhere near enough wood to fill the stove for tonight and tomorrow morning.

"What would you do with a gun?" Ria yelled at them.

"I was itching to kill those two soldiers this afternoon." Dirk looked at her.

"I'm dying to kill those stinking Nazis."
Bram kept aiming his branch.

Dirk had placed his in the bucket.

Ria shook her head. Sometimes boys
could be so stupid. Dirk might think that
he was all grown up, but she knew better.

"See you tomorrow!" Bram hurried to
the gate.

Dirk didn't answer. In silence he picked
up a piece of bark.

"How can we help get the electricity
back?" Ria asked abruptly.

"What do you mean?" Dirk looked at
her.

"We have to do something, Dirk. Mother
is scared," Ria stumbled.

"I have thought about it." Dirk stopped
in front of her. "There's nothing we can
do, Ria!"

Ria swallowed and her eyes filled. She
stomped away. Her brother was all talk
about guns and killing soldiers. She wanted
to help Mother and the new baby.

Gripping the handle of the basket, Ria

marched until she came to the path that wound around the edge of the park. The gravel hurt her feet. Every now and then she had to stop and empty her shoes of the small stones they gobbled. She would not find any wood here, but on she stumbled.

Shivering in the fierce wind, she kept walking until she found an old tree stump. She placed her basket on the ground and sat down. Her thoughts took her back to a long time ago, before the war, when she still went to school. When she had adventures with her best friend Rachel. When in the spring the two friends found the fattest tadpoles in these ditches, while their mothers sat on the bench and talked.

Rachel's Locket

Two summers ago, Ria and Rachel had brought a picnic basket and a blanket to the park. They had pretended they were in a faraway country. The meadows were carpeted with red and white clover and yellow buttercups. Braids undone, the two girls had decorated their long hair with crowns made from daisies. They had pretended to be princesses as they danced barefoot on the soft grass.

Ria and Rachel had been best friends since kindergarten. Rachel had a little brother, Jacob. They lived on the other side of the park, on Chestnut Street.

One day Rachel wore a yellow star on her coat.

"That's pretty," Ria had commented. "Why are you wearing a yellow star?"

"All Jews have to wear one," Rachel had answered.

Ria knew Rachel was Jewish. "But what does wearing a yellow star have to do with being Jewish?" Ria didn't understand.

"The Germans make all Jews wear this yellow star on our coats, so they can recognize us," Rachel said in a tight voice. "Hitler hates Jews. He says Jews are the cause of all the trouble in the world."

Ria couldn't believe it. "Just because you go to the synagogue instead of a church and celebrate different holidays and traditions, Hitler hates you?" She shook her head. How could Rachel and her family cause trouble? They were the kindest people

Ria had ever known.

"Hitler hates Jews," Rachel said again. Her voice quivered.

Another day Rachel came to class in tears. "The Nazis have taken Father's shoe store away." Her sobs came in long gulps. Mrs. de Boer pulled Rachel onto her lap. Ria held her hand. She didn't know what to say to her best friend, but the anger toward the Germans built in her chest.

"Father said we will have to leave soon." Rachel looked at Ria, fear in her eyes.

Every day Ria and Rachel played, while Rachel's parents made plans to find a hiding place in another part of the country. Some days they played at Ria's house and some days at Rachel's. Ria wished Rachel didn't have to go into hiding.

But one day Rachel didn't show up for homeschooling.

"Is Rachel sick?" Ria asked Mrs. de Boer. Then she noticed the woman's swollen, red eyes and the silence of her classmates, sitting around the kitchen table.

"Last night the soldiers came to Rachel's house." Mrs. de Boer's voice was flat. She stared at the kitchen table.

Ria gasped. Fear trapped her breath.

"The Germans came with military trucks," Mrs. de Boer continued. "They took the whole family. Rachel. Little Jacob. The parents." She paused. "Their neighbor told us this morning. He saw everything. They couldn't even take a suitcase. Just loaded in a truck like cattle."

"Where did they take them?" The words burst from Ria's throat.

"Nobody knows." Mrs. de Boer clasped her hands together.

"They take them to camps in Germany and Poland," Bram blurted out. "There they work as slaves or get ... get —"

"Bram!" His mother cut him off. " You listen too much to grown-up talk. Remember the little ones." Her eyes looked at the pale faces around the table.

Ria cried softly. It couldn't be true. It couldn't!

After school she ran to Rachel's street. Her eyes were dry now, but inside she cried. Perhaps it was all a mistake. Maybe in a couple of days, Rachel and her family would be back.

Their house stood quiet as if it were waiting too. Ria walked up the steps to the front door. She did not knock as she had always done. Instead, she pressed her ear against the door. No laughter sounded from the hallway. No footsteps on the stone floor. She sat down on the steps for a moment. Something shiny caught her eye. Ria crouched down, reached into the grass and closed her fingers around a cool object with round edges.

Rachel's locket! Ria cradled it in her palm. Had Rachel dropped it for her to find?

Slowly, Ria walked home. She felt the smooth metal of the locket in her hand.

With tears in her eyes, she showed her mother.

"I'll save it for Rachel," she whispered. "I'll save it for when she comes back."

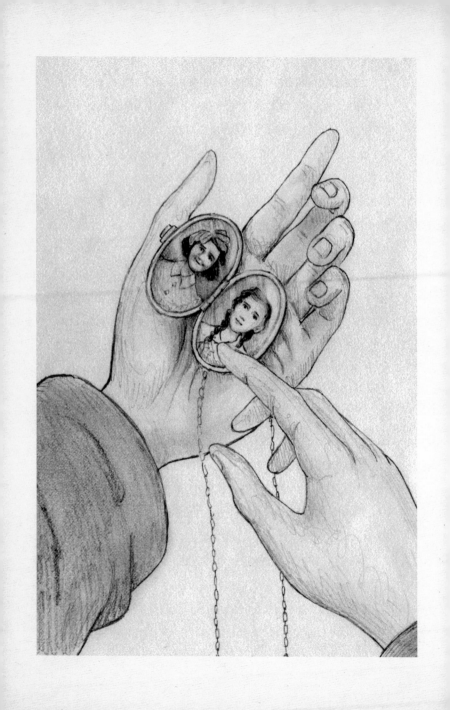

Mother had held her close. They sat in silence for the rest of the afternoon.

★ ★ ★

Now, Ria pulled the gold locket from underneath her sweater. She took off her worn mittens. At one side of the oval locket was a little clasp. The locket opened on a hinge to reveal two tiny photographs. Both were pictures of Rachel. In one she was four years old. Her long, black ringlets were tied in white ribbons. Her wide smile reached her eyes. Ria touched the picture with her finger.

The picture on the other side had been taken just before the Germans came.

In that picture Rachel did not smile.

"Oh, Rachel. Where are you?" Ria whispered. Her eyes filled with tears.

Ria stared out over the wintry land. A crow sat on a wooden fence.

"Do you know where they were taken, Mr. Crow?"

Her throat closed. She had not heard from Rachel. She did not want to see the pictures of Rachel and her family that flooded into her head. She pushed them away. Far away.

But the two Rachels in the photograph still stared up at her. Ria snapped the locket shut.

"Ria! Ria!" Dirk's voice, shouting from afar, brought her back to the park. The cold had made her body stiff as a frozen doll.

She tucked the locket back inside her woolen sweater. The cold metal burned against her skin.

Ria clambered up from the stump. In the distance she saw Dirk. Her movements startled the crow.

She shielded her eyes and watched as the bird flew freely, black against the winter sky.

Ria picked up the basket and waved at Dirk. He came running toward her.

"Mother will be worried. What were

you doing? There's no wood over here!"
he scolded. Ria just let him talk. He was
like an old motor, going on and on.

She followed Dirk home. He was worried
too, she thought. Worried about Mother,
the baby, the cold house and the lack of
electricity.

And about Father being found by the
soldiers.

Home School

"Ria! Hurry!" Dirk stood at the back door.

Ria hugged her mother tightly. "Will you be all right without us? Maybe I should stay with you."

"I won't hear of it. You'll be back at twelve. That's only three hours." Mother chuckled. "You and Dirk are turning into worriers. Go." She pushed Ria toward the door.

Brrr. The December wind blew right

through Ria's clothes. She ran to catch up with Dirk. It was a fifteen-minute walk to the de Boer's place. They crossed the bridge over the canal and followed the dirt road to the farm.

Two years ago, when the Nazis had taken over their school to house soldiers, Bram's mother had become their teacher. The class had started with twenty students, but the group had gradually dwindled. Some parents who owned farms or small businesses kept their children home to help. Other children had been sent away to stay with relatives. And others ... Ria paused. Others were in hiding or, like Rachel, had been taken away.

"Come on, slowpoke," Dirk grabbed her coat sleeve. "Do I have to pull you?" His eyes smiled in his frozen face. "We'll be getting snow." He pointed at the dark clouds racing overhead.

As they crossed the bridge at the turnoff to the de Boer farm, they saw Bram. He waved urgently.

Ria and Dirk sprinted toward him.

"What's up?" Dirk called over the roar of the wind.

"Special mission!" Bram yelled back. "Dirk, Ria, stay with me! We have to make sure the coast is clear!"

"Clear for what?" Ria gasped, out of breath.

"Clear of Germans, of course!"

Why did Bram always have to talk to her as if she were stupid?

Ria clamped her jaws together. Bram had been her classmate since kindergarten. His hair seemed to grow in every direction. Eyes as dark as coals sparkled in his freckled face.

"I can't tell more than that," he added.

Ria and Dirk nodded. They understood.

Every morning, Ria and the other children attended school in Bram's mother's kitchen from nine to twelve. Most mornings were normal, but sometimes mysterious things took place. Some days they were sent out to play and watch for any Germans on the road. Sometimes they heard noises upstairs. Ria knew that Bram's family often helped people hide from the Nazis. Upstairs in the farmhouse were secret places where people hid for short periods of time. Nobody talked about it. Mrs. de Boer always pretended she didn't hear anything.

"All I'm going to tell you is that they're using the car today."

"Who and how?" Ria's heart skipped.

"If you won't tell."

"No. Of course not." Ria took a step closer. Bram had not held onto his secret for long!

Excitement shone from his dark eyes. He looked around and lowered his voice. "My father and Klaas will be dressed in German uniforms. Klaas is the chauffeur."

"But your brother is only sixteen. He can't drive a car." Ria's heart pounded wildly. "And where did they get the car? And the fuel?"

"You haven't told anyone else, have you?"

Dirk looked intently at Bram. "You have to watch it. You could cause your family real danger when you start blabbing!"

Bram's face colored bright red. "I haven't told anybody! Mother just asked if you two could watch out with me."

"We will," Dirk said.

"We have our car hidden in an amazing place." Bram's voice was softer. "We steal the fuel back from the Germans all the time. It's easy. You just siphon it out of their vehicles when they're not watching. I've done it myself."

Ria wanted to wipe the smugness from his face. "I don't believe you. You're bragging, Bram de Boer."

A distant rumble distracted them.

"Look! A truck's coming this way!" Bram's face turned serious. "Quick, Ria! Run to the house and tell Mother!"

Ria's eyes narrowed. A dark vehicle was headed for the turnoff to Bram's farm.

"Don't just stand there! Go!" Dirk took her by the shoulders and turned her in the direction of the farmhouse. As if something had hit her, she shot away. She ran without looking back, expecting to hear the truck coming up behind her at any second.

As Ria neared the farm, the door opened. Mrs. de Boer stood in the doorway, watching Ria anxiously.

"A truck is coming," Ria gasped.

Mrs. de Boer disappeared into the house instantly, closing the door behind her.

Ria waited. The first snowflakes hit her flushed face. As her breathing evened, she realized that the truck was gone. It must have gone on into town. She trotted back down the road.

Bram and Dirk were running toward her. Bram yelled, "Tell my mother the coast is clear!"

Ria retraced her steps to the farmhouse. Again, Mrs. de Boer opened the door before she could knock.

"The coast is clear." Ria repeated Bram's words.

For the second time Mrs. de Boer disappeared inside.

Once again, Ria waited on the steps. Moments later, she heard an engine start behind the barn. She held her breath as a shiny, black car rolled around the side of the barn and passed right in front of her. Inside were two men in German uniforms.

Behind her, the door opened. Mrs. de Boer joined her on the steps.

"Be safe," she whispered after the car. Her eyes misted as the outline of the automobile faded into a curtain of blowing snow.

"Come inside." It had seemed for a moment as if she had forgotten Ria, but now she was herself again. "We'll start with spelling today. The other children are in the kitchen."

Ria followed the tall woman into the house. Her hair was as red and curly as Bram's, but she held it together with a large clasp, inlaid with pearl.

Ria took off her wet outer clothes and joined the students in the warm farm kitchen.

Bram and Dirk came in through the side door. Bram's older brother, Klaas, was the only one missing. He hardly ever attended classes anymore. Today, Ria knew why.

Nel, Bram's fourteen-year-old sister, was clearing away the breakfast dishes.

After greeting everyone, Ria, Dirk and Bram took slates and slate-pencils from the sideboard. They joined the others around the table. The large kitchen stove glowed with warmth. Ria noticed a bucket filled with logs beside the stove. She knew that people who received help from Bram's family often paid with food or fuel. A pot of soup simmering on the stove filled the kitchen with the comforting smell of boiled potatoes, cabbage and turnip. In a basket on the other side of the stove lay the orange tabby, curled up and happy.

Marijke sat thin and shivering beside the stove. Sietske, who had just turned seven, sat beside her. They didn't talk.

Next to the girls sat Jaap, his head shaved. He must have had lice again. The thought made Ria's head feel itchy. On the other side of the stove sat Nynke and Johannes, sister and brother, who lived north of town. Their father had been a teacher at Ria's school, but he had been sent away to Germany to work as a slave. Ria felt a wave of fear as she watched the two siblings. At least her father was still with them, even though he had to hide from the Germans day and night.

"Ready?" Mrs. de Boer looked around the circle. "I'll start with grade one. H-o-u-s-e," she spelled deliberately.

It wouldn't be her turn for a while. Ria's mind wandered. What if she went to city hall herself and asked the mayor about the electricity? A chill ran down her spine at the thought. How would she get in? Could she just walk into the building? What if it were guarded? And the mayor? He must like what the Germans did or he wouldn't be mayor. What if he asked her about Father? After all, look what the Germans had done to Rachel!

She looked at Bram. He was staring out the window. His mind must be wandering too.

"E-s-p-e-c-i-a-l-l-y! Ria! Bram! Pay attention!"

Ria jumped. Her slate slid off the table and broke in two.

Ria's Plan

Ria was almost out the door when Bram called after her. He was pulling his coat off the hook in the kitchen.

She paused. What did he want now?

"I'll walk with you. I'm going into town."

Ria's eyes widened. "But I'm going home. I need to check on my mother."

"Well, we still go the same way as far as Canal Street," he said, walking past her out the door. Ria followed, but Mrs. de

Boer's voice stopped her.

Bram's mother had stuck her head around the door. "You let me know if your mother needs anything, Ria. And Bram, pick up those socks from your grandmother." Snow blew in the door around her feet.

"We need electricity," Ria said.

"I know," Mrs. de Boer answered. "Those Nazis have no mercy. They just had to cut the power right before Christmas. People are freezing in their own homes. Tell your mother I'll come by tomorrow. I'll send Dirk home shortly," she added. "He agreed to do some chores for me now that the men are gone."

Ria turned to go as the door closed behind her.

As she caught up with Bram, the wind almost pushed her past him.

"Will your father and Klaas be safe?" Ria asked.

"We won't know until they come home. If they come home." Bram paused. "If they get caught, the Germans will shoot them on the spot."

"Don't you dare remind me how terrible the Nazis are!" Ria shouted. "You are lucky. Your father's a farmer. He doesn't have to hide from the Germans!" The unfairness of the situation almost choked her. "Why are you coming with me, anyway?" She looked at his red face.

"I know you don't like me." Bram stopped, blocking Ria's path. "You think I'm only bragging. But I've done important stuff for the resistance." His eyes looked straight into hers.

Ria knew he wasn't kidding. His whole family was involved. She nodded.

Bram looked away. They walked on in silence. Just before the bridge, Ria said, "Do you know what the mayor is like?" As soon as she said it, she regretted her question. Bram would make fun of her, or worse, blurt it out to somebody.

"He's enormous." Bram stretched his arms. "Tall," he added. "And strong. But worst of all, he is a Dutch Nazi. Why do you want to know?"

"I … I want to talk to him." Ria looked straight at Bram.

"Why do you want to do that?" He grabbed her sleeve.

Ria paused. She hadn't really thought it out. "I have to help my mother," she said softly. Her eyes filled up. "She's scared. She's going to have her baby soon and the house is cold and dark. And my father has to hide."

"I know." Bram did not laugh.

"I thought I would go to city hall. If I could speak to the mayor, maybe he would give back our electricity. At least for a while."

"I don't see how that could work," Bram said slowly. "The mayor doesn't have that much power. He obeys the Germans. He doesn't care about us." He still held onto her sleeve. "All the mayor does is make sure that German orders are being followed."

"But he could help us," Ria said. She swallowed. "Did he agree that the order should be followed to pick up the Jews in this town?"

"Yes," Bram said. He let go of her sleeve. "Even if he didn't agree, he wouldn't have a choice. But I bet he agreed. He's a stinking Nazi collaborator."

Ria stared at the road. Her thoughts turned fast.

"I'm going to city hall right now to check it out."

Bram looked at her. His mouth opened as if to speak.

"Yes," Ria said. "I need to make a plan. I can't just walk in the door and talk to the mayor. I've heard there are guards at city hall."

"That's right." Bram looked at her. "The resistance broke into city hall and stole food coupons and blank identity cards. That was a good thing, but now the building is guarded day and night. You'll never get past those guards."

Snowflakes melted on Ria's hot face and sent tiny rivers inside her coat collar.

She would show him! She would get past those guards.

Ria turned left onto Canal Street. Her hands stuffed deep in her pockets, her face determined, she strode away from Bram.

"Ria! I'm coming with you!" He jumped in front of her. "You're only nine!" he blasted in her face.

"So are you!" Ria yelled back. She pushed him aside.

Bram didn't answer. Ria walked briskly away from him. Her heart beat fast, pounding with anger and worry for her mother and with fear of the mayor and the German guards.

Bram followed her down Canal Street, where bridges crossed the canal to the other side. People hurried by, shivering in the cold afternoon. Half walking, half running, Ria and Bram turned right on Main Street. A large army truck bore down on them. Ria felt the roar of the engine in the pit of her stomach. Bram stayed right behind her. She gasped for breath. A sharp pain stung her side.

All of a sudden Bram grabbed her coat. "Wait."

Ria looked at him. His deep frown told her he was thinking hard.

"If we stay on this side of the road, we'll have a good view of city hall."

Ria agreed. "But they can see us too. I'm going behind the shed of this red house," she said. "You don't need to come with me. I'll just check things out."

Bram stayed right behind her until they were out of sight and sheltered by the shed's overhanging roof. From there they could see city hall, the tall, white building with concrete steps going up to a double oak door. Two white pillars held up the tiled roof.

The snow had turned to sleet. The dampness reached Ria's skin through her worn clothes.

"See those two soldiers beside the door?" Bram said. "They are the problem. You have to get past them."

"But I can't. They'll see me as soon

as I walk up the steps."

"You have to get behind the pillar and sneak inside when they're not watching."

"That's never going to work." Ria walked away from the shed. "I have to go home!" She had forgotten about her mother, but now the image of Mother's face, scored with deep worry lines, pushed everything else aside.

"Let's do it now!" Bram's voice was harsh. "Your mother needs electricity NOW! Not next week. We have to act fast."

Listening to Bram's voice turned Ria to ice. She couldn't do it. It was impossible. And she didn't want Bram here with her. It was her idea.

"No, Bram," she said. "I have to have a good plan."

Bram persisted. "We can get closer when we walk on this side of the road where the trucks are parked. We'll hide beside the fourth one and watch how long the two guards stay."

Ria didn't like the idea. And she didn't

like being pushed around by Bram. Still, not sure why, she followed him.

As they neared the fourth truck, Bram stopped. "Soldiers," he whispered." They're in the truck. We can't hide now."

As he spoke, the engine started. Black exhaust spewed from the rear of the truck, choking them. Ria covered her face with both hands. The tires groaned and the truck moved away, leaving Bram and Ria in clear view of the guards at city hall.

Ria watched as the two soldiers noticed them.

The next moment they came running down the steps. Panic rose in Ria's chest.

"You two! What are you doing there?" one of the soldiers shouted.

Bram swore. He grabbed Ria's hand. Her feet stuck to the ground. He pulled her hard back toward Canal Street.

Fear didn't hit her full force until she heard running boots pounding behind them. Close to the corner, Bram pulled her behind a house.

A dog barked. Startled, they climbed a fence.

Ria was sure she could hear the soldiers right behind her. She kept running. They stumbled through a vegetable garden, clambered over tree stumps and followed an overgrown path. They ran without looking back.

A man with a shovel blocked their way.

"What are you two doing here?" His wool cap was pulled over his ears. "You are trespassing!" His voice was gruff.

Ria and Bram stopped, almost choking. They gulped for air.

The man stared at them.

"Soldiers," Ria said between breaths. "Soldiers are chasing us."

"I don't see any soldiers." The man looked beyond them. "Nobody is following you."

Ria slowly turned. She had been sure that the two soldiers were breathing down their necks. It was a relief to discover that the man was right.

"They had guns." Bram had finally found his voice.

"What were you two up to?" The man chuckled. "Soldiers just don't chase kids for fun."

"We only looked at them," Bram said.

"Yeah, sure." The man shook his head. "If you keep to the left and follow the path beside that brick house," he pointed his shovel at a yellow house, "you will come out on Canal Street. You'd better go home and not look at soldiers again." He shook his head once more.

Ria looked at Bram.

He nodded.

Much calmer, but with her heart still beating wildly, Ria led the way to Canal Street. They walked in silence. Every now and then Ria looked over her shoulder to make sure they were not being followed.

Each time a military car or truck passed by she cringed. What if the soldiers had gone back and asked for help in the search?

Ria shivered. She didn't think she would

have the courage to go to city hall again.

Close to her turnoff at Park Street, they stopped.

"Don't give up yet," Bram said. "We'll try again tomorrow!"

"No, Bram," Ria said. "It's too dangerous. Too impossible."

"Think of your mother. You can't let her down."

"I know," Ria said softly. "I have to go home now."

"Will you think about it?" Bram turned.

Ria did not answer right away. The encounter with the soldiers still shook her.

Then, "Don't forget to go to your grandmother!" she said. "And Bram?" She took a deep breath. "I will think of a good plan."

Getting Organized

After the evening meal, Ria, her mother and father huddled around the kitchen table close to the stove. The small stove made clinking sounds, but gave off little heat.

The air was thick with moisture from the laundry that hung from clotheslines strung from wall to wall.

Three bricks lay side by side on top of the stove. Later the hot bricks would warm their beds. Ria wore her winter coat.

Mother had wrapped herself in a blanket.

The blackout curtains were pulled down, making the house pitch black. The Germans made everyone use blackout curtains. They checked that no light could be seen from the street. Ria didn't like the blackouts. They made the house spooky and scary.

A howling wind made the family shiver in the poorly heated kitchen. They stayed alert to outside sounds. Every time a car came down the street, Father jumped up and got ready to go to his hiding place.

Dirk wore his gloves and sat on a bicycle that was strapped onto wooden blocks. He pedaled to keep the bicycle's light burning. Ria held a tiny dynamo light. Squeezing the lever made it light up. As soon as she let go, the light turned off. Ria and Father would take turns on the bike as well.

"We need to get organized for this new little person." Mother rubbed her belly. "Could we bring one of the beds downstairs?" She looked at Father. "At least here in the kitchen there is a little warmth."

"Take my bed," Ria offered eagerly. "I can sleep on the spare mattress on the floor."

"Tomorrow I'll bring the kerosene lamp and fuel from farmer Piet," Father said.

"I can't have people pedaling for light during the delivery. And I'm nervous about burning candles while the baby is being born." Mother looked at everyone's face. "What if they get knocked over and the house burns down?"

"The bicycle won't fit in the kitchen when we bring the bed down, anyway." Father looked around the room. "We'll just have to be careful. Piet's lamp will help. The biggest challenge will be getting water to boil on this stove." He added softly, "When your mother starts labor, Dirk, you go get Nurse Bettie. If it's after curfew, you will have to be careful not to be seen."

Ria hoped that Mother would go into

labor during the day instead of at night. It scared her to think of Dirk sneaking along pitch dark streets, avoiding the soldiers.

"I'll hide behind houses and sheds in the dark alleys," Dirk said.

Dirk was brave after all. Ria's heart started to thump. She thought of what she and Bram had done this afternoon.

Dirk took his feet off the pedals and Ria let go of the lever of the dynamo light. The room grew instantly dark. Ria stood. It was her turn to pedal.

"Couldn't we go to the mayor and ask him to give us the electricity back?" she asked suddenly. Her face burned. It was easier to say the words in the dark. She mounted the bike and started to pedal furiously.

"Nobody," Father's voice rose, "I said nobody is going to set foot in city hall. Is that understood?" He looked at Dirk and then at Ria. "We do not trust the mayor. He is the enemy. Such a reckless action would put us all in danger." His voice became softer. He took Mother's hand.

"How will we get word to you if I start labor during the day?" she asked.

"It will be Ria's job to come to the farm and tell me." He smiled. They sat for a while listening to the wind.

Mother yawned. "It's not getting any warmer in the kitchen. Let's go to bed."

Father helped her up. Ria wrapped the bricks in towels and gave one to Dirk and one to Father.

Dirk pressed the small dynamo light and guided the family up the stairs.

Ria's bedroom was ice-cold. The floor felt like a skating rink under her feet. Groping around in the darkness, she found her bed, pulled back the covers and shoved the brick into the spot where her feet would find warmth. Then she climbed in herself and made a tent of the blankets. Only then did she take off her coat and cardigan. She wore her pajamas under her sweater and kept her stockings on. Even bundled up like that, she did not get warm for a long time. Under her pillow, she found her old, stuffed rabbit, the rabbit her grandmother had made out of soft pink flannel when Ria was just a baby.

Sleep didn't come. Ria rubbed her feet together on the warm brick. She rolled onto her side, pulled the covers over her head and snuggled the rabbit in her arms.

Even when she started to get comfortable, her mind kept racing. She could not let go of her promise to Bram. The promise to come up with a good plan. Now, added to that was her father's warning that if anyone went to city hall the whole family would be in danger.

Despite his words, Ria felt that her mother needed her to take the chance. But how? Try as she might, she could not think of a way to get into city hall on her own. She needed Bram to help her. And what if they got caught? Would the Germans take them away, like Rachel's family? She couldn't think about that. But she could not just stand by and do nothing. Her mother was frightened. Ria felt for the locket, which she wore even at night. Her fingers closed around it.

"Oh, Rachel, what should I do?"

When sleep finally came and took her far away, Ria dreamt she was looking for electricity. She was carrying a long cable. Every time she came to one of the big hydro poles, she climbed to the top and fastened the cable. But there were so many poles. And the cable grew heavier and heavier.

Finally, she reached the last pole, the one nearest her home. Her mother stood in the doorway yelling, "Hurry, Ria! Hurry! The baby is coming!"

Ria started to climb the last pole. All of a sudden a voice barked, "Halt!"

A soldier with a vicious face stood at the bottom of the pole and pointed an enormous rifle at her.

"No!" Ria woke with a start. She sat up. Her hair was wet. Her heart beat fast against her ribs.

The room was pitch black. Her breathing was uneven. Slowly bits and pieces of the dream came back to her. She thought about it for a while, hugging her stuffed rabbit tight. Her mind worked its way around to the two guards on either side of the door at city hall and her decision to talk to the mayor. Could Bram distract the guards? In her semi-dream state, a plan came to her. Bram could draw the guards' attention by siphoning gasoline from one of the trucks right in front of them. The thought of the guards running after Bram in their black boots brandishing their guns woke Ria up completely. She sighed. That would be too dangerous. Bram might get caught.

Scared

Ria looked at their big grandfather clock.
It ticked steadily.

"Meet me at the corner of Main and
Canal Street at three," she had whispered
to Bram when she was bundling up to
go home after class that morning.

"I know how you could distract the
guards," Ria had said. It was a dangerous
plan, but it was the only one she had.
She had decided to see what Bram thought

about it.

"What do you want me to do?" Bram had whispered back.

Ria told him her idea. Bram nodded, showing no doubt or hesitation. And Ria joined Dirk who had waited outside.

Now, at home, they ate the noon meal in silence. It was potato soup and soggy bread, which Dirk had bought with the bread coupon at the bakery this morning. They were lucky that Father brought fresh milk from the farm every day. They always let the milk stand overnight. In the morning it was topped with a rich layer of cream. Every day, Ria scooped off the cream into a glass bottle. She shook the bottle, singing "Churn butter, churn," until the cream turned into chunks of yellow butter floating in sour whey.

Ria helped clear the table. Mother looked tired. Tomorrow was New Year's Eve. The baby could come at any time.

She helped her mother upstairs and tucked her in.

Later, Dirk and Ria pulled on their threadbare coats once more. They went to the park to scrounge for firewood. The wind swept their faces and whipped their cheeks.

Ria scrabbled for tiny bits of wood. She even pulled roots and dead grass and collected a few crunchy leaves. Her feet and hands were numb from the cold. Pretty soon there would be nothing left to burn in the stove.

"Hey!" A tall boy with a black toque called from the other side of the path. "Dirk, come here. I need to talk to you!" His voice barely reached them through the roar of the wind, but Ria recognized Jan, Dirk's friend.

She collected more twigs while Dirk talked to Jan.

"Can you take the wood home?" Dirk asked Ria. "I'm going with Jan to help his father in the store."

Ria nodded. She lugged the basket and Dirk's bucket home.

It was almost three o'clock.

Ria told Mother that she was going to help Mrs. de Boer for a while. She hated lying to her mother. At least Dirk wasn't there, asking questions.

"Don't stay too long," Mother said. "It's getting dark already." She closed the door behind Ria.

Ria ran. Her legs moved as fast as they could pushing against the wind. Once on Canal Street, she slowed down.

She needed to stop, to gasp for air. Traffic was busy. Military trucks, jeeps and soldiers on bicycles roared along the street in both directions. Her heart drummed hard in her chest. It was much better to walk than to run, she thought. She wouldn't attract as much attention.

Ria followed Canal Street until she reached the corner of Main. The sky darkened. The wind seemed angry, she thought. Whiffs of wood smoke from nearby houses filled her nostrils and made her cough. A woman with two crying children walked ahead of her. She sauntered behind them.

In front of the red brick house on the right, stood Bram. He leaned against the fence, a metal bucket in his hand.

Ria walked up to him. "Are you ready?" Her voice wavered.

Bram nodded and pulled a piece of rubber hose from his pocket.

"This is what I use to siphon gas. And look." He nodded in the direction of city hall. "At least five of those monsters are parked along the street in front of the building."

The first truck blasted its horn.

They watched as a funnel of black smoke spewed into the street and the vehicle began to move toward them.

Ria shivered. What if the soldiers from yesterday recognized them? She made herself skinny, hoping the Germans in the truck wouldn't notice her.

"Let's go." Bram looked at Ria's tight face.

"I don't know, Bram." Ria stood still.

"What if it doesn't work? What if they catch you?"

"I'm quick," Bram said, but his voice was shaky. "Remember I've done this many times."

Slowly, they walked in the direction of city hall. They met an old man pushing a wheelbarrow, a boy on a bicycle and two women carrying a large box. Ria looked at the houses on either side of the street to see if Bram could get away if he had to.

They had almost reached city hall when a soldier crossed the street toward them. Bram pulled Ria back. They scurried behind one of the big tires of a truck. Ria's heartbeat matched the stomping boots. They stayed hidden until the soldier passed by.

Crouching down, they walked beside the two trucks until they were straight across from city hall.

Bram peeked around the front of the truck. "It looks good," he said. "There are no guards at all." He pushed Ria in front of him. "When I say GO, you run behind the pillar on the right."

Ria's heart pounded in her throat. What were they doing? It was too dangerous. She knew that. And what if her father were right?

Bram broke into her thoughts, "If any soldiers show up, I'm ready to distract them." He held up the tube and the bucket and grinned. "For now I'll hide behind the same shed as yesterday and wait for you."

Ria didn't move.

"You have to, Ria." Bram's voice was in her ear.

Ria couldn't think. She just nodded.

As soon as the road was clear, Bram pushed her. "GO!" he whispered.

Ria ran across. She climbed the big, concrete steps.

She had just reached one of the fat, white pillars, when two soldiers marched out of the building. They stationed themselves on either side of the heavy, oak door.

Ria flattened herself against the pillar. Her heart beat hard in her chest.

She held her breath and peeked at the soldiers. What would they do if they found her? Would they lock her up? Send her away?

Her hand touched the locket safely tucked inside her sweater.

What if Bram couldn't get their attention? What if he changed his mind? She shouldn't have listened to him. She was stupid. What if the soldiers stayed beside the door all afternoon? I'll never be able to get inside, she thought.

Ria stood like a statue, concealed by the fat pillar, listening. Every now and then she glanced out at the soldiers.

The wind howled. The cold crept through the cardboard soles of her shoes.

Ria waited, her heart caught in her throat.

"HE! WAS MACHST DU?" The soldier's voice startled her. Screaming and waving their rifles, the soldiers ran down the steps

together. Ria's body turned to stone. Bram, she thought. They've seen him and they're going to get him.

Not letting herself think, she dashed to the door. She turned and saw the two soldiers grab Bram.

"NOOO!" His scream of rage and fear pierced her heart. But there was nothing she could do to help Bram. Her job was to see the mayor. Her stomach twisting, she squeezed inside.

The bright light of the chandelier hanging from the ceiling of the large entrance hall blinded Ria's eyes. Of course city hall would have electricity! The light was so bright, they could easily spare some for her family.

Near the door four plush chairs with burgundy stripes were grouped around a low, wooden table. Loud voices approached. Ria dove behind one of the chairs.

"Morgen früh um sechs, werden wir de Boer's Bauernhof, östlich vom Kanal, durchsuchen."

From her hiding place, she listened carefully. Ria didn't know much German, but she understood the words *morgen* (morning), *durchsuchen* (raiding), *Bauernhof* (farm) and she recognized the name "de Boer." They were going to search Bram's farm. She had to warn his family.

Ria listened for more words but the voices had disappeared into one of the rooms on the left. Peering out from behind the chair, she spotted a sign on a door that said 'MAYOR.' The door was quite a distance away, where two hallways met the big lobby.

A door opened.

Ria felt for her locket. She squeezed it hard.

Heavy boots strode toward her. She kept her head down, afraid to look. The floor trembled under those boots and so did Ria.

The sound of the boots passed outside.

Ria listened. Any moment she expected

the soldiers to come back, dragging Bram with them.

Not a sound.

Taking a deep breath, Ria ran for the door with the big sign. She opened it, but froze on the spot. Footsteps came running from the left. A hand grabbed the collar of her coat.

"HEY! HOW DID YOU GET INSIDE?" a voice hollered.

The Mayor

Ria struggled to keep her feet on the ground. She found herself looking straight at a man who sat behind a large desk. He wore a brown suit and glasses and had a bushy moustache.

"Who do we have here?" his voice boomed.

The mayor, Ria thought. Even in a suit, he looked as frightening as the Germans in their uniforms.

"You can put her down now, Franz."

The soldier behind her let go of Ria's collar. Her legs almost buckled beneath her.

"You can go," the mayor said to Franz. "I can handle this intruder myself. If she poses any danger, I will call you. Stand outside the door."

"Yes, Herr Mayor."

Ria stood and stared straight ahead. She heard the man leave and the door close.

"Sit down," the mayor said in a kinder voice.

Still shaking, Ria made her way to the big, leather armchair across from the mayor and perched on its edge. He looked at her. Ria looked at him. For a terrible monster he had kind eyes, she thought. The room smelled of cigar smoke. Behind the mayor, on the wall, hung a large painting of Hitler. On the corner of the desk stood a picture frame, and a red and white flag with a black cross with hooks on each bar. A swastika.

"What is your name?" The deep voice startled Ria.

"Ria." She paused.

"Well, Ria, for a little girl, you have great courage. You walked right into this building even though it is full of soldiers. You snuck by the guards and now you have bounced right into my office without so much as a knock!"

Ria's face colored.

"I suspect you have something of great importance to tell me."

Ria's heart pounded.

"It … it is of great importance," her voice quivered. "My mother is having a baby."

"THAT'S what you came to tell me?"

"No! No!" Ria's eyes filled with tears. "Mother's having a baby and we need light and a heater and … We need electricity. But you cut us off." The words rushed out. "And yesterday …" Ria looked at the mayor. "Yesterday, soldiers came to the house. And … and they stole my mother's tin candleholder." Ria shifted on the edge of the chair.

"We *need* electricity for when the baby comes," she repeated. Involuntarily, she felt for the locket. "My mother is so tired and scared. The baby might die. You have to help us! You have to talk to the Germans!" She forced herself to look at the mayor's face.

The mayor looked at Ria.

Her hand twisted the locket under her sweater.

Finally, he spoke. "When is this baby due?"

"Now! Today! Tomorrow! I don't know!" Ria swallowed.

The mayor picked up the picture. He looked at it. His eyes softened. He came out from behind his desk and handed the picture to Ria.

She looked at the photograph. It showed a girl with blond braids, about her age. The girl's face smiled at Ria.

"That is my daughter," the mayor said. He was smiling too. "Her name is Greta.

She is nine."

Ria looked at the face in the picture. "I'm nine-and-a-half," she said proudly.

"She lives with her grandparents, down south." The mayor took the photograph from Ria and placed it back on his desk.

He cleared his throat. "I will look into the matter. But I cannot promise anything. We need the electricity. There is not enough fuel." He stared at Ria. "What is your address?"

Ria trembled. Father would not want her to tell him where she lived. But how else could the electricity be connected?

The mayor waited.

Ria swallowed hard. "I live at 56 Park Street."

The mayor took a pencil and wrote on a piece of paper. "You may go now."

Ria slid off the chair.

"Franz!" the mayor called.

The door opened and the soldier rushed in. He looked young, but his eyes were cold.

"Make sure this young lady gets outside safely."

"Yes, Herr Mayor." The soldier clicked his boots together.

"You'd better hurry, Ria. It's getting dark."

Ria hesitated. She wondered if she should ask the mayor about Bram. But maybe Bram had gotten away. And the mayor could not yet know what had happened.

"Ria!" He dismissed her with a nod.

Franz's hand gripped her shoulder, pushing her down the hall. He opened the door. Ria tried to shake his hand off, but he grabbed her coat.

"Go home!" he yelled and gave her a shove.

Ria almost tumbled down the concrete stairs. Her eyes scanned the street. There was no sign of Bram.

Shaking all over, Ria crossed the road. She ran behind the house with the shed, where Bram had said he would wait for her. She knew she would find no one there.

"Bram!" she called. Her voice shook. She tried the wooden door, but it was locked. She knocked on the walls. "Bram!"

A sickening feeling overwhelmed Ria. She sagged against the wall of the shed.

They had taken Bram. First Rachel, now Bram.

The Lost Locket

Ria walked down Main Street. Every now and then she looked behind a house or a shed. There was no sign of Bram. Just as she thought, the soldiers must have taken him. For one moment she wondered if she should go back to city hall and ask the mayor about Bram. But the memory of Franz's hand on her shoulder made her cringe. She couldn't do it. She concentrated on hoping that Bram had gotten away.

The wind had died down. Charcoal clouds flocked the darkening sky and dropped soft, feathery snowflakes on her hair and her face. In no time, her coat was covered with white lace. Ria started running. She shielded her eyes with one hand. There were no streetlights. Two trucks drove by, but Ria hardly noticed them. The houses had pulled down their blackout curtains. Her shoes were soaked. The cardboard soles opened and closed, flapping with every step she took.

On Canal Street, she slowed down, wondering if she should go home or to the farm, to find Bram. What would she tell his parents? Mother would be worried, too.

What had she done? Her stomach churned. She should have listened to Father.

When she turned onto Park Street she began to run. The snow came down hard now. Ria shivered. Her coat soaked up the flakes as they melted. The dampness crept through her woolen sweater and reached her skin.

Exhausted, she fell against the back door of their shed. Footsteps sounded from inside. The door opened.

"Ria!" Mother's voice pierced the air.

She grabbed Ria's arm. "Where have you been?"

"I ... I ...," Ria gasped, her cheeks burning, "I saw the mayor."

"You did what?" Mother pulled her inside. She closed the door. It was dark in the shed. Mother opened the door to the kitchen. "Here she is." She handed Ria to her father.

"Where have you been? What was that you said about the mayor?" Father took her shoulders.

"I asked the mayor for electricity. But Bram ... Bram helped me ... The soldiers took Bram!"

Dirk jumped up, almost sending his chair over. In the middle of the kitchen table stood a bowl filled with oil and a wick. The wick burned, spreading a dim light. The table was set for the evening meal.

Father held onto her arms and looked closely into her face. "What have the two of you been up to? I told you never ..." He turned toward Dirk. "Run to de Boer's farm and find out what happened to the boy!"

Dirk was already throwing on his coat. He grabbed his toque.

"No!" Ria said. "I must go. I heard something at city hall."

Father's voice was louder than usual. "What did I tell you last night? Now, you have gotten us all into trouble! As well as Bram's family."

"No! I didn't!" Ria tried to wriggle free of her father's grip.

"The soldiers will come pounding on our door."

"No," Ria repeated. "The mayor said, 'I promise I will look into the matter.'"

"The mayor will never do that, Ria." Mother's voice was hoarse with worry.

"Can you hold the baby in, Mother?"

"Don't believe the mayor, Ria. He is a Nazi sympathizer, remember?" Then a faint smile touched her mother's pale face. "Our baby won't wait. When it's time for this baby to be born, it will come, electricity or not."

"What did you overhear?" Dirk stood, all bundled up now, and looked at his sister.

"Father! Mother! I have to go to the farm." Ria looked from one to the other. "I have to!"

"No!" Father let go of Ria's arms. "You stay home." He walked over to his wife and guided her to the chair beside the stove. "Dirk can tell them what you overheard."

"I heard, 'morning, raiding, de Boer's farm,'" Ria felt sick. She had a vision of the de Boer family being loaded onto a truck, just like Rachel's family.

Father walked over to Dirk. "Tell them they're going to be searched in the morning. Hurry!"

The kitchen door clicked shut. The outside door banged.

"Let's sit down." Mother's bottom lip

quivered. She poured Ria a glass of milk. The three of them sat at the table.

Father sliced the bread, but no one ate. In the dusky kitchen they waited for Dirk to return. It seemed to take forever. Father and Mother were silent. Ria's mind went around in swirls. Whatever she had thought was the right thing to do this afternoon, now seemed to be all wrong. She felt sick if she thought of Bram. Where had the Germans taken him?

A commotion at the back door startled them. Mother stood. Ria jumped off her chair and opened the kitchen door.

Dirk burst inside, breathing hard. "He's not home!"

Ria gasped.

"Oh, no!" Mother clasped her hands. "Those poor people. They do so much to help others. Ria, how could you?" Tears ran down her face.

Father's face had turned an ashen gray. "You warned them about the raid tomorrow morning."

"Yes." Dirk hung up his coat. He walked to the stove and held his hands against the kettle.

"What are they going to do about Bram?" Ria's voice quivered.

"Wait," Dirk turned to look at her. "All they can do now is wait, till he comes back or ..." He did not finish his sentence, but Ria understood.

Finally, they sat down at the table, but nobody touched the food. Doubts, fear and guilt closed Ria's throat.

"I can't believe you went." Dirk broke the silence. "What did he say to you? The mayor."

"He was nice to me." Ria was not going to tell him that she had almost died of fright when the soldier had grabbed her by the collar of her coat. "He has a daughter. Her name is Greta. She is nine."

Mother looked up.

"He misses his daughter." Ria looked at her plate.

"Nice?" Dirk's voice strained with tension.

"Did you know that he didn't do any-thing to stop the Germans from deport-ing all the Jews in this township?"

Ria nodded. A lump filled her throat.

"Did you tell him about our family? Mention Father?" Dirk's voice was tight.

"No. Only that we needed electricity for our baby." Ria didn't look at her parents.

"Did you give him our address?" Father raised his voice.

"Yes," Ria nodded meekly. "He needs to know which house so he can connect the electricity."

"But they can't just connect one house, can they?" Dirk looked at Father.

"They could," her father answered. "But it would be a lot of trouble. They would have to reconnect the whole street, then take all the fuses out, except ours. They will never do that."

"Oh, Ria." Mother swallowed hard. Her hand rested on her stomach.

Ria started. "Is it coming now, Mother? Do you have the cramps yet?"

"No. No, Ria. I'm just so worried about what you did. Maybe your father should hide under the stairs tonight."

Oh, no. Ria didn't want her father to be all cramped and cold. It had been such a good idea. But the more she looked at the worried faces of her parents, the more she felt it had been wrong. Bram was gone and she had put her family in danger.

Later, in the coldness of her room, Ria slid beneath the covers, fully clothed. Fear, heavy as a rock, had settled in her chest. She pulled the covers straight over her head. And felt for the locket.

Her throat was bare.

She jumped out of bed and stumbled downstairs. Dirk sat at the kitchen table working on an old puzzle. Mother unraveled something white.

"What's wrong?" Father, pedaling on the stationary bike to keep the light burning, looked at her horror-stricken face.

"I lost the locket." Her hand was at her throat.

"Oh, Ria," Mother's eyes filled.

"I lost Rachel's locket," she repeated desperately.

"When did you lose it?" Her father stopped pedaling and reached for Ria. She pressed her face into his woolen sweater.

"I have to go back to city hall," she whispered.

Without the light from the bicycle, the room was dark except for the small wick on the table. He tilted Ria's chin and looked into her face. "Are you sure you lost it there?"

"I'm almost sure. The last time I felt it was in the mayor's office."

"You could have lost it on the way. Or here at home," Dirk said.

Ria shook her head. "I remember twisting it around when I sat in front of the mayor's desk. I have to get it back," she sobbed. "It belongs to Rachel. I was saving it for when she comes back."

"I know." Father stroked her hair. "But you can't go back to city hall, Ria. It's too dangerous. None of us can go. Next time the mayor might not be so kind." Father wiped the tears from Ria's face with his big, red handkerchief.

Ria looked at her family. "I was scared," she admitted. "I hate those Germans with their angry faces, stomping boots and barking voices."

"We're all scared, Ria," Mother said. "We cannot risk trying to get Rachel's locket back."

New Year's Eve

Ria shivered. During the night her thoughts had gone from Bram, to Rachel's locket, to her father, sitting in the cramped, cold space under the stairs. Now, silently, she walked beside Dirk. A thin layer of snow covered the gravel road to the de Boer's farm.

When the farm came into view, Ria's heart sank. What if Bram wasn't home yet?

The farmhouse was silent. Dirk rang

the bell. They heard footsteps.

Mrs. de Boer opened the door. Ria looked into her pale face.

"Come." She ushered them inside. "Go straight to the kitchen. Never mind the mess. We had visitors."

Ria's heart felt cold as she followed Dirk.

She gasped when they entered the kitchen. Two chairs lay in pieces beside the wood stove. A bucket filled with broken china stood beside the sink. Nel was busy organizing the drawers of the sideboard. There were no children.

"School has been cancelled," Mrs. de Boer said. "Sit down. I'll pour you some warm milk."

"Mrs. de Boer, I don't need milk. I'm sorry about Bram. I ..." Ria gripped the back of a chair.

"It's all right, Ria." Mrs. de Boer put her hand on Ria's arm. "Bram is home."

Ria swallowed hard. "Where? Where is he?"

"Come with me." She took Ria's hand

and led her toward the door to Bram's parents' bedroom.

"He might be asleep," she whispered. "The doctor gave him something for the pain."

The heavy curtains were drawn. Mrs. de Boer left the door open behind them. She walked Ria to the side of the bed.

"Bram," Ria whispered. All she could see was a mop of red curls on the white pillow.

"Yeah," Bram said, pulling the covers down. "They got me."

Ria looked at his swollen face. Her stomach turned. "Oh, Bram."

"They kept me in a dark room at city hall all night. They asked me questions."

"That's enough." Mrs. de Boer took Ria's hand and pulled her away.

"Ria ..." Bram's voice was weak.

Ria stopped.

"Did you get the electricity back?"

"No," Ria said. "It was all for nothing." Tears ran down her face.

Mrs. de Boer put her arm around Ria and guided her into the kitchen. Dirk stood beside the stove talking to Nel.

"It was not for nothing, Ria." Bram's mother handed Ria a handkerchief. "Thanks to you we were able to get a Jewish family with two children to safety."

Ria looked up.

"If you hadn't overheard what the Germans said yesterday at city hall, we would all have been shot. Early this morning at five, three army trucks drove up to the farm. At least twenty soldiers." Mrs. de Boer paused. "They searched the whole house, the barn and the stables. They made a mess in every room. But thanks to you, they didn't find anybody." She placed her arms around Ria and hugged her tightly. "Bram came home after the raid. They were hoping that Bram would tell them about the people we were hiding." She wiped her eyes with a tip of her apron. "We are very proud of Bram. He didn't tell them anything." A thin smile lit her face.

"And now you two better go home and look after your mother. Here." She opened the pantry. "I have some candles, and someone gave me some real cocoa."

★ ★ ★

Darkness had fallen. The kerosene lantern that Father had borrowed stood on the table. Ria and Dirk worked on an old puzzle they'd had for years. Father read a book. Mother knitted. The table had been pushed against the wall. Ria's bed had been brought down to the kitchen and stood beside the stove. A small electric heater was plugged in underneath the window just in case the electricity was reconnected.

The light from the lantern cast a soft glow over their faces. When they moved, their huge shadows shifted on the wall.

"Can we stay up till midnight?" Dirk looked at Father. "It's New Year's Eve."

"No, Dirk." Father shook his head. "We don't have enough fuel to burn this lamp for that many hours."

"Why don't I make that hot chocolate you brought home from Mrs. de Boer?" Mother put her knitting on the table and rose from her chair. She could barely squeeze through the space between the bed and her chair.

Ria's and Dirk's eyes gleamed. "We haven't had hot cocoa in ages."

"Well, it's a special night." Father smiled.

Ria tried to think of the last time she'd had hot chocolate. Then, she knew. At Rachel's house. It was a bittersweet memory because it had been her second-to-last visit with Rachel. She thought about the locket she'd lost yesterday. On the way back from the de Boer's farm, Ria and Dirk had searched for Rachel's locket along Canal Street, but they hadn't found it. Ria had been too afraid to search Main Street.

Dirk helped Mother with the hot chocolate. "Mmm." The rich smell tickled her nose.

Steam rose from her cup. Ria stirred and smelled. She closed her eyes, concentrating on the thick, chocolate aroma. Her mouth watered. She took a tiny sip and savored the liquid in her mouth for a long time.

"I'll make a toast," Father said. "Even though it isn't midnight. Everyone raise your cups. The year 1944 has come to an end. We hope that 1945 will bring us," he looked at Mother and smiled, "a healthy baby and PEACE."

They all touched cups.

"I'm so glad we're all safe." Mother's eyes misted. "They didn't come looking for Father. Bram's family is safe and so is the family they were hiding."

In silence, the four of them drank their hot chocolate.

"Your mayor didn't keep his word, Ria." Dirk put his cup down. "What else could you expect from a dirty Nazi collaborator."

"Shush." Mother warned him with her eyes.

Ria refused to look at him.

"We won't talk about it anymore." Mother gathered the cups. "Here Ria, you take them to the sink. We'll manage without electricity."

Ria looked at her mother. She was bundled up in three sweaters, which hardly covered her swollen stomach. Ria had hoped fervently that the mayor would help them, but he had not.

Dirk picked up a puzzle piece and snapped it into place. Ria didn't feel like helping him anymore.

"Aah," Mother cried out.

"Mother!" Ria jumped from her chair bumping into the bed. She looked at her mother's twisted face. Her father had risen too. Dirk's face was pale.

"Does it hurt?" Ria stared at her mother. Mother smiled weakly.

"I wish the mayor had kept his promise," Ria said. "Now our baby will be born in this dark, cold kitchen." Her eyes filled with angry tears.

Dirk remained silent.

A new wave of pain hit their mother. She braced herself against the bed. Ria took her hand. Father stroked her hair. Mother gripped Ria's hand so hard it hurt. Ria's heart skipped. She was afraid. Why did the baby have to be born right now, tonight, in the dark? Why had the mayor refused his aid?

When the pain passed, Mother smiled weakly at her family. "It feels like this baby is coming fast."

"Where are you going?" Ria's father had grabbed his coat.

"Dirk. Get ready," he ordered. "You go and fetch Nurse Bettie. I'll see if the doctor is home. Ria," he grabbed her shoulders. "You take good care of your mother until I come back. Start heating water."

Ria nodded.

Dirk hurried into his own coat. Curfew or not, no matter how many soldiers were out there, they had to get help.

When her father and brother had gone,

Ria flicked the light switch. She must have checked it a hundred times today. Nothing happened. The room stayed dark. Ria sighed. She grabbed the kettle and filled it with water from the pump. Before she placed the kettle on the stove, she added some logs that Father had brought home from farmer Piet.

"You should get into bed," Ria said. She grabbed her mother's hands again when she noticed she was having another contraction.

After the pain subsided, Mother said, "Please get the baby's basket and the towels from upstairs."

Ria let go of her mother's hands.

"Here, take the lantern. I can sit in the dark for a few minutes."

Ria walked quickly up the stairs. In her parents' bedroom she found the wicker basket that was made up as a baby's bed. She placed the towels on top, and carried the basket under her arm.

Back in the kitchen, she placed the

baby's basket close to the stove.

"Hang the blankets over the clothes-line above the stove, so they can warm up." Mother's breathing was uneven.

Mother and Ria waited. The pain came and went. Every time a new wave hit her mother, Ria squeezed her hands. In between contractions, she checked on the water, the towels and the blankets and got the candles from the front room. Mrs. de Boer and the neighbors had generously shared their limited supply of candles. Ria put tiny baby clothes on top of the kettle.

A commotion at the back door announced Dirk's return. Nurse Bettie, the midwife, was with him. She hung up her coat and sat down beside Mother. "I would feel much better if you went to bed," she said. "Those contractions are coming too fast for you to be sitting around here."

Ria helped her mother undress and handed her a flannel nightgown.

Father opened the door. "I got more

wood. Can you help me, Dirk?"

Dirk went into the shed.

Moments later Father carried a load of logs into the kitchen and stacked them beside the stove. He turned to the bed and put his hand on Mother's arm. "The doctor is out," he said quietly. "There was an accident."

Waiting

Ria and Dirk sat and listened, shivering at the top of the stairs. Nurse Bettie had sent them firmly to bed.

"You will stay in your rooms, well out of the way," she had said, shooing them up the stairs.

At first they'd each gone to their rooms, but Ria was too excited to stay cooped up alone. She knocked on Dirk's bedroom wall.

"I'm not going to bed," she called. "I want to wait up."

Dirk opened the door between the rooms. He held the small dynamo light in his hand. "Come in here," he said. "We can wait together."

In her pitch-black room, now lit by the thin ray from Dirk's light, Ria pulled one of the blankets off the mattress on the floor. She draped it around her shoulders and followed Dirk into his bedroom.

The light danced on the walls, giving glimpses of posters of airplanes.

Settled on the bed, wrapped in blankets, they listened. They waited.

Mumbling voices came from below. Someone opened the squeaky door of the stove. They heard the clanking of logs on metal.

The door at the foot of the staircase opened. Ria recognized the sound of Father's feet on the stairs.

She slid off the bed and opened the door. Dirk was right behind her.

"Father?" Ria touched his arm. "How is Mother?"

"She is doing her best. Nurse Bettie said it won't take long."

"Can we see the baby?" Ria shivered.

"I know it's cold up here, but I'll get you as soon as the baby is born. I promise." He planted a kiss on her forehead, turned and went downstairs.

The cold forced them back under the blankets. Ria yawned. She opened her eyes wide. She was not going to fall asleep.

Shivering, she rocked on the edge of Dirk's bed. "What is taking that baby so long?"

"I don't know." Dirk pointed the dynamo light at the posters on the wall. He shone the light up and down a Lancaster, one of the British bombers. The ones they often heard in the middle of night. These planes flew over from England and dropped their bombs on Germany. He moved the light to a picture of an RAF pilot standing beside a Spitfire.

Finally, Ria could stand the waiting no longer. Quietly, she opened the door. She could hear a variety of sounds including mumbling voices, but no baby crying.

"Let's wait at the top of the stairs," she said.

Dirk sat down beside her and pulled a blanket around the two of them.

"What time is it?" she asked.

Dirk shone the light at his watch. Their grandmother had given it to him after Grandfather Dirk had passed away.

"Ten to twelve." Dirk sighed.

"Do you think our baby will be born this year?" she asked.

"I don't think so."

They stayed silent. They listened.

"I'm sorry the mayor didn't help us," she said.

"Bram's family certainly was happy that you went and overheard the Germans." Dirk yawned.

Then, "Wow!" they yelled together as

the bulb on the ceiling blazed into light.

Ria squeezed her eyes shut and opened them again. The upstairs was bathed in bright, yellow light.

"The mayor kept his promise!" they both screamed.

"Father! The lights!" Ria called.

The door to the stairs opened. Father's head came around the corner.

"The mayor kept his promise, Ria," he laughed. "Just hang in a little longer." Then turning back to the voices in the kitchen, "Yes, I'm coming."

They now heard Nurse Bettie's and Mother's voices full of excitement.

Ria grabbed Dirk's hand. She laughed and cried. "I think it's coming." She moved down one step, pulling the blanket with her.

"Hey!" The blanket forced Dirk to follow. "We can't go down. Nurse Bettie won't let us."

"I know. I'm almost bursting. I can't wait anymore."

Dirk laughed. "You have to."

Finally, the door opened and a tiny wail rose up the stairway.

"THE BABY!"

Father stood at the bottom of the stairs. "You may come down, now," he said. His face glowed. His eyes shone with tiny, sparkling stars. His smile looked as big as a slice of the moon.

Daughter of Light

"Oh, Father. That's our baby crying! May we see the baby?" Ria and Dirk tumbled down the stairs, almost tripping over the blanket.

"Yes, Ria. Your smart little sister waited to be born until the electricity was switched on."

He opened the door wide to let them into the softly lit kitchen. The warmth from the stove and the electric heater embraced Ria's chilled body.

Nurse Bettie had just bundled up something little that squealed and was handing it to Mother. Ria stared at the small bundle. She made her way to the bed through the crowded kitchen.

Father helped Nurse Bettie gather up the sheets and towels.

Slowly, Ria inched closer, her eyes never leaving the bundle in her mother's arms. She felt Dirk right behind her.

The room smelled of antiseptic and ... baby.

In the soft light, Mother's face was radiant. "Come closer, you two," she smiled.

Ria and Dirk stood beside the bed.

Mother moved the baby blanket aside. Dirk and Ria gazed down at their new sister. Ria couldn't speak. Her throat closed. She just looked.

"Come," Mother said. "Pull up a chair and you can hold her."

Ria's heart beat so fast, she could hardly bear it. She sat down and reached out

her arms. With great tenderness, Mother handed her the baby.

Ria bent over and peered at the red, wrinkly face. Her sister's features twisted and grimaced. A tiny fist appeared from under the blanket and searched for a mouth.

Ria touched the soft cheek with a fingertip.

Father stood at the foot of the bed, smiling. "So what do you think of our little miracle?"

Ria smiled back.

"What's her name?" she asked softly.

"We will call her Annelise," Father said. "It means graceful light. She is our daughter of light."

Mother touched Ria's face. "Thanks to you, brave daughter." Mother's eyes glittered and her face shone.

Ria's heart beat against her sister's tiny body. She stroked the dark, damp hair.

"Listen, Annelise," Ria whispered, "soon this war will end. We will plant new trees in the park and make it beautiful again.

We will never again be cold. We will never again sit in the dark."

Annelise's tiny face stretched and yawned.

"And we will never, ever have to be afraid of bad soldiers. They will all be back in Germany where they belong."

Annelise made smacking sounds, and Ria brushed her cheek against the baby's soft skin.

She wished she could hold the baby forever, but Dirk wanted to hold her too. Ria placed her carefully into his waiting arms. Dirk's hand supported Annelise's tiny head. His face turned bright red when she squirmed.

"I hope she's not scared of her big brother," Ria chuckled.

"I hope she doesn't have to listen to the two of you bickering," Mother laughed.

Father went to the front room to get the camera. Since the war had started, they had stopped taking pictures. You couldn't buy rolls of film or photoflash bulbs. There were only a few pictures left.

"This is a special moment." Father laughed. "Sit closely together," he ordered. Ria perched on the bed and threw her arms around her mother. Dirk held Annelise. They all smiled at the camera.

Pop. The little light bulb flashed a tiny jolt of lightning. The picture was taken.

Nurse Bettie turned from the sink, where she was putting laundry in a large kettle. "Time to give your mother and sister some rest," she said.

Ria and Dirk said goodnight, and kissed their mother. Gently, Ria pressed her lips to Annelise's forehead.

"Goodnight, Annelise," she whispered.

An Unexpected Visitor

The days that followed were filled with extra chores and visits from friends and neighbors.

"You're the only people in town who have electricity," Mrs. de Boer said. "What a luxury!"

Homeschooling had resumed right after New Year's Day, but Ria and Dirk stayed home to help their mother. Every morning, Nurse Bettie came, but only for an hour.

Father had put up extra clotheslines all over the house. Coming inside the kitchen, they had to make their way through the hanging diapers.

Bram came to visit every day and so did his mother. They brought eggs, milk, potatoes and cabbage. Bram's eye had turned from black to yellow. The swelling in his face was almost gone, but he still limped.

After the midday meal, Ria, Bram and Dirk went to the park, scrounging for wood, twigs and pieces of bark. The lights and the electric stove were still working, but they knew that wouldn't last.

The cold had turned the water in the canals to ice. All were anxious to get their skates on.

"Do you think we will be able to keep the electricity?" Dirk carried the basket.

"Maybe the mayor has forgotten that you have it." Bram pulled his toque over his ears.

"I don't think so." Ria thought for a

minute. What if the mayor expected her to return and tell him that their baby was born? She shivered. No, she wasn't going back to city hall. She would never again visit the man who had done nothing to prevent Rachel's deportation. But he had reconnected their electricity. Maybe she should go back. No, he had probably only helped her because she reminded him of his daughter, Greta. But maybe someone in city hall had found Rachel's locket. Her thoughts circled like a merry-go-round. She felt for the empty spot beneath her sweater.

"Oh, Rachel," she whispered. "I can't believe I lost it. Where are you? I wish you were back. What would you think about the mayor giving us electricity? Helping us, but not helping you because you are Jewish?" Ria pushed that question away. It was too hard to think about.

"We have enough wood for today," Dirk said, leading the way out the gate.

Ria waited for Bram to catch up. He

took his time and she noticed the grimace in his face every time he moved his right leg.

She felt bad for Bram. He had been so brave to draw the attention of the soldiers away from her.

They couldn't cross the road. Four army trucks with soldiers roared down the street. Bram and Ria stopped beside Dirk. Ria stopped breathing. Dirk placed his arm around Ria's shoulder. Ria grabbed Bram's hand. Were they heading for a round-up somewhere? Had they learned of people in hiding?

The trucks passed. Ria let go of her breath, but she couldn't stop trembling. They held onto each other as they crossed the street, walking slowly for Bram's sake. He gave Ria a big smile. "A few more days and my leg will be fine."

"It must hurt a lot." Ria bit her lip.

"Yes, it does," he said quietly. "But, Ria, what we did was good. Good for the people we were hiding. Good for my family.

And good for yours." His eyes sparkled. "As soon as I can run again, I'll continue my fight. You can help! We'll distribute illegal newspapers. I'll teach you how to siphon gasoline. And maybe we can come up with a plan to blow up all those trucks."

Ria's laugh bubbled. "Yeah, right, Bram." But she liked the thought of helping, of doing something against the Nazis.

"I know," he said. "I'm bragging."

Ria didn't answer. She just smiled.

That evening, Ria and Dirk worked on the puzzle they had left unfinished on New Year's Eve. One thousand small pieces would make a picture of a castle, with high walls and a drawbridge.

The bed had been moved back to Ria's room. The kitchen felt less crowded.

Father read an illegal English leaflet that Dirk had brought home from Bram's family. The leaflets had been thrown out of Allied planes. Everyone listened when Father explained that the Allied troops were making progress to liberate their country. After he'd finished reading it, he threw the paper in the stove.

"The Nazis don't want us to read these," he said. "They don't want the Dutch people to find out how badly the German armies are losing."

"How far away are the Allied armies, Father?" Dirk looked at his father.

"They are fighting hard, but the Germans are holding out at the three great rivers."

"I know they'll beat them," Dirk said with confidence.

"Yes, they will," Father agreed.

Ria felt warm inside. She could hardly wait for the Germans to leave. She thought about the mayor. What would happen to Nazi collaborators when the Germans lost the war? Would he go home to his daughter?

The next day Ria and Dirk were busy helping their mother. Ria couldn't believe how many diapers a little person like Annelise dirtied in one day. They all had to be washed by hand.

That night the family sat around the table again. Ria looked at each in turn. Dirk was reading a book. Father was fixing a table lamp and Mother was nursing Annelise. The light above the table still shone brightly. Ria wondered, once again, how long the Germans would let them keep the electricity.

The sound of a car driving down their street made them all freeze.

"GERMANS!"

Father stood up and gathered his tools, his jacket and his cap. Mother buttoned her blouse. Dirk opened the door to the stairs and lifted the loose boards. Father crawled into his hiding place.

They all heard the car stop, the car doors slam.

Moments later, there was a pounding on the door.

Ria, Mother and Dirk jumped.

"Dirk, close the door to the stairs. Here!" Mother placed Annelise in Ria's arms.

The pounding continued.

Ria couldn't breath. Were the Germans coming for her father again?

As soon as Dirk had closed the door to the stairs, Mother went into the hallway.

She turned back and took Dirk's arm. "You come with me."

Oh, please. Don't let them find Father. Fear made Ria's stomach clench. She held Annelise closer.

A strangely familiar voice filled the front hall. "I came to see that important baby of yours." An enormous man strode into the kitchen, his tall frame filling the room. Mother and Dirk followed him, looking bewildered and scared.

"I also brought you candles." He turned to Ria's mother and handed her a box of utility candles. "You will need these when we cut your electricity again."

The mayor looked at the baby in Ria's arms. He stroked her wispy hair.

"What's your baby's name?" he asked Ria. His eyes twinkled.

"Annelise," Ria said proudly. "It means

graceful light."

"That name is perfect." The mayor laughed. "Well, little Annelise, you are lucky to have such a brave sister." He reached inside his overcoat, then held his hand out to Ria. Something glistened in his palm.

"The locket!" Ria gasped. "Rachel's locket." Tears welled up in her eyes.

Mother took Annelise from her arms.

The mayor smiled and handed Ria the gold locket.

"The other day at my office, we talked about something of great importance. After you had left I found the locket under my desk. Greta has one exactly like it." Ria felt his eyes on her hot face.

The mayor touched his felt hat, turned and left the room. They listened as the car rumbled away down the street. For a long moment, only the ticking of the wooden clock on the wall disturbed the silence in the room.

Dirk opened the door to the stairs, took out the loose boards and helped

Father squeeze out of his hiding place.

Ria looked at him with smiling eyes.

At that moment, the light switched off. The room turned pitch black.

Annelise started to cry.

"It's all right. It's all right." Ria could hear her father fumbling in the dark. He lit a match and took one of the candles the mayor had brought.

In the soft glow of the candlelight, Ria opened the locket. Rachel looked up at her out of the photograph. How could it be that the same man who had done nothing to stop the soldiers from rounding up Rachel's family had returned Rachel's locket?

War did not make any sense.

"Please, Rachel, come back," she whispered. "Let me show you our Annelise, our daughter of light."

Historical Note

Daughter of Light is a work of fiction. The town and the characters in the story are all fictional, but the events are based on historical fact.

In 1933, the Nazi Party, led by Adolf Hitler, took power in Germany. Hitler and his party believed that the Germans were part of a superior race. They believed that Jews, gypsies and disabled people were to blame for Germany's poor economic conditions and therefore should be eliminated.

The Second World War began in September 1939, when Germany invaded Poland. The following spring, the German armies took over Norway, Denmark, the Netherlands, Belgium and France. German troops landed in the Netherlands on May 10, 1940. The Dutch armies fought hard, but after the Germans bombed the seaport of Rotterdam the Dutch army surrendered.

During the five-year occupation, the Dutch made do in tough circumstances. Food rations, curfews, blackouts and raids were commonplace. The Nazis took over many buildings, such as hotels and schools, to house their soldiers.

Jewish people were singled out for persecution. Every aspect of their lives was controlled. They were not allowed to enter public buildings or parks or to take public transportation. They lost their businesses, their jobs and their homes. They were forced to wear a yellow star on all their clothing. Many Jewish people went into hiding. The Nazis held raids to round up Jews, who were loaded onto trains and sent to concentration camps in Germany and Poland to work as slaves or to die in the gas chambers.

Many Dutch people tried to sabotage the Germans; these people were part of the underground movement known as the resistance. They risked their lives working to save Jews and others in danger from the Germans. Allied pilots who had been shot down were hidden, moved from one safe house to another to escape detection. When possible, they were transported back to England. All Dutch men between the ages of seventeen and fifty-five were ordered to work in the weapons factories in Germany, but many went into hiding.

During the winter of 1944, the last winter of the war, the Dutch people suffered greatly. The weather turned extremely cold and food was in short supply; many people died of starvation that winter. It was during that bitter, dark December that the Germans cut off the supply of electricity. Coal, petroleum and wood had been sent to Germany. People were forced to scavenge for scraps of wood to burn in their stoves. Now they had no electric light, nor could they use their small electric heaters or stoves.

For heating and cooking, many people used a small iron stove called a *rus*. For light they used candles, carbide lamps, kerosene lamps, dynamo lights or bowls filled with oil and a wick. Many people rigged up a stationary bicycle that could be pedaled to provide light. Dynamo lights were small, handheld devices similar to today's flashlights. Instead of batteries, though, the dynamo light lit up when a lever was squeezed.

Siepie de Vries was born on New Year's Eve, 1944; the unusual circumstances of her birth inspired my story. She arrived safely because her father had dared to go to the Nazi mayor of the town to ask if his family could have their electricity restored. In a rare act of kindness, the mayor approved. For three weeks the de Vries family enjoyed the luxuries of electric heat and light and food cooked on an electric hotplate. They were the only non-Nazi family in town to receive this privilege. After three weeks, the Germans cut off their electricity and once more the family coped with cold and darkness. But their baby had been born safely.

For five long years, the Dutch suffered every day. In such trying times, small events like those in this story of light gave people hope.

New teen novel by martha attema - available from Orca Book Publishers Fall 2002

When the War Is Over is martha attema's third teen novel set in the Netherlands. *A Time to Choose* (Orca, 1995) won the Blue Heron Book Award and was a finalist for both the Arthur Ellis Award and the Geoffrey Bilson Award for Historical Fiction. *A Light in the Dunes* (Orca, 1997) was an American Library Association "Quick Pick for Reluctant Readers" and made the New York Public Library Books for the Teen Age list. martha attema lives in Corbeil, Ontario.

Also in the *Orca Young Reader* series:

The Freezing Moon
Becky Citra

In this sequel to *Ellie's New Home*, the year is still
1835. Ellie has learned many of the skills she needs
to survive as a pioneer, but she is plagued by fears.
The true test of her courage comes in the dead of
winter when Papa fails to return from a day's hunting.
Will Ellie be able to overcome her terror, protect her
brother and get help?

Becky Citra, a primary schoolteacher and writer,
lives on a ranch in Bridge Lake, BC, where horses,
bears and coyotes abound and where many of the
chores have changed little since the days of pioneers.

1-55143-181-5; $6.95 CAN; $4.99 USA

Also in the *Orca Young Reader* series:

Jesse's Star
Ellen Schwartz

Jesse is in trouble. His class project is due tomorrow and he hasn't even started.

How is he supposed to know why his ancestors came to Canada? Even his mom can't help him. Jesse's only hope is in the attic — maybe his great-great-grandfather's traveling case will have some letters, passports, or even a diary inside.

But the case contains only an old photograph and a Star of David on a chain. Disappointed, Jesse looks down at the star in his hand.

Now how is he going to find out about his ancestors? Jesse puts the chain around his neck.

And then the star begins to glow.

1-55143-143-2; $6.95 CAN; $4.99 USA

Also in the *Orca Young Reader* series:

The Keeper and the Crows
Andrea Spalding

Misha's Aunt Dora has moved to an old cottage in the historic town of Belfountain, and Misha can hardly wait to visit. But when he arrives, Misha finds that his aunt has also attracted the interest of the local crows, who watch her every move. Odder still, they seem to listen in on Misha's conversations with his aunt. What is going on?

Before he knows it, Misha is drawn into his aunt's secret. She is the Keeper, caretaker of an ancient box of great power. Aunt Dora holds one key to the mysterious box, but the other key has been stolen by the crows. Now the evil birds are determined to find the box and claim it — along with all its powers — for their own.

The crows won't let Dora out of their sight. Now it's up to Misha to search out and reclaim the stolen key.

And he must act alone.

1-55143-141-6; $6.95 CAN; $4.99 USA